The skunk who
stunk

by Rosie Greening

make
believe
ideas

Get the most from this reader

Before reading:

● Look at the pictures and discuss them together. Ask questions such as, "What is the skunk doing here?"

● Discuss what your child thinks will happen in the book and why. Check after reading to see if this prediction was correct.

● Relate the topic to your child's world. For example, say: "What do you do if you want to make new friends?"

During reading:

● Prompt your child to sound out unknown words. Draw attention to neglected middle or end sounds.

● If your child makes a mistake, ask if the text makes sense and allow him or her time to correct it before helping.

● Occasionally, ask what might happen next, and then check together as you read on.

- Monitor your child's understanding. Repeated readings can improve fluency and comprehension.

- Keep reading sessions short and enjoyable. Stop if your child becomes tired or frustrated.

After reading:

- Discuss the book. Encourage your child to form opinions with questions such as, "Did you like the ending? Why or why not?"

- Help your child work through the fun activities at the back of the book. Then ask him or her to reread the story. Praise any improvement.

Skunk was a nice, friendly animal.
There was just one problem ...
he smelt terrible.
Skunk smelt so bad that none of the
other animals wanted to play with him.
It was hard for Skunk to make friends.

Skunk felt lonely. He wished he had someone to play with. "If I smelt nice, I would have friends," he said.

So, Skunk thought of ways
to get rid of his bad smell.

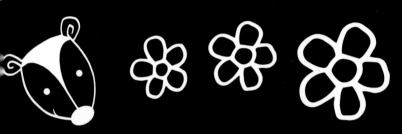

Me + nice smell = friends

Skunk's first idea was to spray
perfume all over himself.
The perfume smelt nice,
but it made him sneeze.

Achoo!

"I'll try something else," said Skunk.

Skunk decided to bake something that smelt good. "Cookies smell better than perfume, and they don't make me sneeze," said Skunk.

The cookies smelt sweet.
The kitchen smelt sweet.
But Skunk did not smell sweet!

15

Poor Skunk had no more ideas. "Will I ever have a friend?" he said.

Skunk felt so sad and lonely that
he decided to cheer himself up.
He went to his favourite place
in the world: the compost heap.

"Everything smells bad here," said Skunk. "I fit in well!"

He headed for the smelliest part of the heap, but then he got a surprise. A black-and-white tail was sticking out of the compost. Someone was sitting in his spot.

It was another skunk, and
she smelt just the same as him.
"Hello! You look nice," she said.
"Let's be friends."
"Yes, please!" said Skunk.

At last, he had a friend who liked him just the way he was. He never tried to change his smell again!

Discussion Questions

1 Why didn't anyone play with Skunk?

2 What made the kitchen smell sweet?

3 How do you think Skunk felt when he found a friend? Why?

Me + nice smell = friends

❧ Sight Words ❧

Learning sight words helps you read fluently. Practise these sight words from the book. Use them in sentences of your own.

his

went

get

but

did

with

again

not

Rhyming Words

Can you find the rhyming pairs?
Say them aloud.

stunk

twice

smell

cheese

nice

skunk

sneeze

tell

mend

sweet

bake

pale

tail

fake

cheat

friend

Read the words, and then trace
them with your finger.

terrible

animals

sneeze

perfume

something

surprise

smelliest

decided

Root Words

Match each word
with its root word.

Root words:

friend
bake
sneeze
smell
cheer
sweet

Words:

baking
smelt
cheerful
friendly
sweetest
sneezed

Words for Comparing

Follow the lines to match each word with its comparison and superlative.

bad

lonely

lonelier

good

nice

worse

nicer

worst

better

nicest

loneliest

best

This book belongs to

. . . .

Copyright © 2021

make believe ideas ltd

The Wilderness, Berkhamsted, Hertfordshire, HP4 2AZ, UK.

All rights reserved. No part of this publication may be
reproduced, stored in a retrieval system, or transmitted
in any form or by any means, electronic, mechanical,
photocopying, recording, or otherwise, without the
prior written permission of the copyright owner.
Recommended for children aged 5 years and over.
Manufactured in China.

www.makebelieveideas.co.uk

Photographs courtesy of Shutterstock.